W9-DHH-447

LADYBIRD BOOKS, INC.
Auburn, Maine 04210 U.S.A.
© LADYBIRD BOOKS LTD 1992
Loughborough, Leicestershire, England

All rights reserved. No part of this publication may be reproduced, stored in a retrieval system, or transmitted in any form or by any means, electronic, mechanical, photocopying, recording or otherwise, without the prior consent of the copyright owner.

Printed in U.S.A.

Scaredy Kitten

By Jane Resnick
Illustrated by Steve Smallman

Ladybird Books

On the night before Christmas, Prescott was all bundled up to go caroling with his sister Sylvia and their friends. He opened the door and peered outside.

Gosh! he thought. *It's dark. Very dark.*

"It's too cold for me," Prescott said to Sylvia.

"It is not," Sylvia said. "You're just afraid of the dark. Scaredy kitten!"

3

Prescott went to his room and took off his scarf and hat and mittens and boots. He put on his pajamas, turned on his night light, and crawled into bed.

"Oh, no!" he said suddenly. "How could I forget?"

He got out of bed and pulled his shade down tight so he couldn't see the night.

Prescott *was* afraid of the dark. He couldn't tell where the darkness ended and everything else began. He felt as if he was disappearing in the dark. And that made him very nervous.

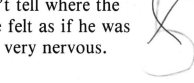

5

Most of the time it didn't matter that Prescott was afraid of the dark. But sometimes it mattered a lot.

On the Fourth of July everyone went to the town green to watch the fireworks. Everyone except Prescott.

"It's too buggy," he said. "I can watch from my window."

"Scaredy kitten!" said Sylvia.

Prescott went to his room and tried to watch the fireworks from his window. But he ended up turning on his night light and pulling the shades down tight to keep out the night. He never saw any fireworks at all.

On Halloween, Prescott wore a ghost costume for trick-or-treating. He thought that maybe the bright white sheet would help keep him from disappearing in the dark.

8

But when he stepped outside, he saw that it was rainy and foggy and *very* dark. *Everything* disappeared.

"It's too wet for me," said Prescott, going back inside.

"Scaredy kitten!" said Sylvia.

9

Prescott stayed inside that night and greeted all the other trick-or-treaters at the door. They were all smiling and laughing. Prescott hid his sad face behind his mask.

A week after Halloween, it was Prescott's birthday. His grandfather came to his party and brought a special present. When Prescott opened the box, he didn't know what it was.

"This is a telescope," Grandpa explained. "You take it outside at night and look through it to see the sky up close. You'll be surprised when you see what's up there. But we have to wait until dark."

14

Prescott didn't want to be surprised in the dark. He didn't want to go outside at night at all.

"Scaredy kitten," whispered Sylvia. "I bet you don't go!"

15

But Prescott loved Grandpa very much, and he couldn't disappoint him. So when the sun set, he went outside into the dark with Grandpa and the telescope. He held Grandpa's hand.

Grandpa showed Prescott how to put his eye to the end of the telescope and look up at the sky. "Just look through it and tell me what you see," he said to Prescott.

17

Prescott looked.

"I see stars," he said. "Oh! Look at them! They're so shiny! And look at the moon! The moon is so bright! It's like a huge flashlight! Wow!"

Prescott was amazed.

When Prescott took his eye from the telescope, the night didn't seem so dark any more.

"Is the moon there every night?" Prescott asked.

"Yes," Grandpa said. "On foggy, cloudy nights you can't see the moon and stars very well, but they're there. You can count on the moon."

20

"I can?" Prescott asked.

Grandpa smiled. "Yes," he said. "I knew you'd be surprised. I'll bet you didn't know there was so much light in the night."

21

When Prescott went to bed that night, he didn't turn on his night light and he didn't pull down his shade. The stars shone in his window and the moon gleamed brightly.

22

Prescott watched the light in the night glowing in his room.
And he wasn't afraid of the dark any more.